A VISIT FROM DR. KATZ

Atheneum Books by Ursula K. Le Guin

The Tombs of Atuan
The Farthest Shore
Very Far Away From Anywhere Else
Leese Webster
A Visit from Dr. Katz

A Visit from Dr. Katz

by Ursula K. Le Guin

illustrated by Ann Barrow

ATHENEUM   1 9 8 8   NEW YORK

Atheneum, Macmillan Publishing Company, 866 Third Avenue, New York, NY 10022
Collier Macmillan Canada, Inc.

Type set by V & M Graphics, New York City
Printed and bound in Hong Kong
Typography by Mary Ahern
First Edition

10 9 8 7 6 5 4 3 2 1

Library of Congress Cataloging-in-Publication Data

Le Guin, Ursula K.   A visit from Dr. Katz.

SUMMARY: Although Marianne is sick and has to stay in bed, she is cheered up by medical
treatment from her two cats.
[l. Cats—Fiction. 2 Sick—Fiction] I. Barrow, Ann, ill. II. Title.
PZ7.L5215Vi   1988   [E]   87-1783
ISBN 0-689-31332-2

When Marianne gets the flu, and feels bad and has to stay in bed, she says, "Do I *have* to?"

Her mother says, "Yes, you have to."
Then Marianne feels like crying, and says, "*But . . .*"
And her mother says, "Now you just lie down,
and I'll see if Dr. Katz will come in and see you."

Then Marianne lies quietly waiting, and soon
she sees Dr. Katz coming in.

Dr. Katz comes in on eight white paws, and goes two different directions. Dr. Katz has long, white whiskers.

One of Dr. Katz is Philip.

Philip comes over to the bed, jumps up onto it, walks up across Marianne's stomach, looks into Marianne's eyes, and says, "Prrrrrrr."

Marianne sniffles and smiles. "Hello, Doctor!" she says. "You're wearing a beautiful fur coat."

She strokes his beautiful fur coat.

She sniffles again and tells him, "I feel bad, Doctor. I have to stay in bed all day!"

Philip does not blink. He gazes at her, then turns around three times on her stomach and lies down with his paws curled under his chest.

Marianne can feel him purring, and her stomach begins to get nice and warm.

"That feels good, Doctor," she says. "It must be the Stomach Cure."

Meanwhile, Philip's little brother Lorenzo, who is called The Bean, is walking around Marianne's room smelling the legs of chairs, tasting eraser crumbs,

crawling under things,

leaping over things,

and exploring the top
of Marianne's desk.

finding out what is
in the wastebasket,

By the desk is a window, and outside the window
is a sparrow. The Bean makes a noise like a toy
machine-gun at the sparrow: "Ch-ch-ch-ch-ch-ch!"

"Doctor!" says Marianne. "You didn't come
here to hunt birds!"

The sparrow flies off. The Bean turns around,
sits down on a school folder, and gazes at
nothing.

"Doctor!" says Marianne. "I'm over here!"
The Bean pays no attention.

Marianne wiggles her toes.

The Bean looks at the two bumps that Marianne's feet make under the blankets. The bumps wiggle. The Bean crouches down—his tail lashes—and he pounces on the wiggling feet.

He chews Marianne's toes through the blanket.
This tickles, and makes Marianne laugh.

"Oh, Doctor," she says, "this must be the Toe
Cure. Do I have the flu in my toes?"

The Bean looks wise, but does not answer.

He finishes chewing Marianne's toes and then walks slowly up her legs until he comes to his brother Philip. He walks across Philip and stands on Marianne's chest.

He looks into her eyes and says, "Prrrt-mee?"

Marianne scratches him under the chin until
his nose points straight up into the air.

After that he lies down partly on Marianne and partly on Philip, and begins to wash Philip's neck.

Marianne strokes Dr. Katz's backs.

Philip wakes up partly and begins to wash The Bean's right hind leg, which is under his nose.

The Bean washes Philip's left ear.

Philip washes The Bean's tail.

"I'm getting left out of this!" says Marianne. She scratches Dr. Katz gently under the ears, and both Dr. Katz wash Marianne's hands.

Then they each wash one of their own paws, slowly.

"Doctors are always very clean," Marianne tells Dr. Katz.

They look at her with their golden eyes and
smile. They know.

After a while Marianne's mother looks in.
Marianne and Dr. Katz have all gone to sleep.
One of them is still purring.